Fairytales Retold: The Golden Bird

Fairytales Retold: The Golden Bird

Avril Sabine

Cracked Acorn
Productions
Australia

Fairytales Retold: The Golden Bird

Published by

Cracked Acorn Productions

PO Box 1365

Gympie, Queensland 4570

Australia

978-1-925131-54-3 (Kindle)

978-1-925617-31-3 (EPUB)

978-1-925131-87-1 (Large Type Print)

Genre: Fairytales Retold Short Story

Cover design by Caitlyn Petersen

As the head gardener, Lenard's father must find out who is stealing the fruit from the king's golden apple tree. Neither of his older brothers have been able to discover the culprit and Lenard wants his chance to prove himself. Instead his family continue to treat him like the sickly child he once was. Someone needs to solve the mystery because no matter how great a king is, it's never good to fail them.

*

People have been telling stories since the beginning of time. Fairytales, folklore, myths and legends are among some of the stories that have been told over and over through the centuries. The basic story remains the same, but each storyteller adds their own style, sometimes adding something unique to the tale.

*

This story was written by an Australian author using Australian spelling.

The Golden Bird

Lenard tried to ignore the mocking laughter of Norbert and Harriman, his older brothers, as he spoke to Ritter, his father. "At least give me a chance." He gestured towards his brothers. "They each had their chance. I won't fall asleep like they did."

Ritter slowly shook his head. "I'm going to have to tell King Alfred I'm getting too old to be his gardener. I barely manage to stay awake till ten each night. Staying awake the entire night to catch some thief is beyond me."

"You can't." His father had worked in the Royal Gardens his entire life. He'd be lost without his job. He eyed Ritter. When had his father's black hair and beard become more grey than coloured? Even his shoulders no longer seemed to be as broad as they'd once been. "Wait one more night. Let me try and catch the thief."

"Think you're better than us, do you?" Norbert demanded.

Lenard tried to think of a reply that wouldn't set his older brother off. At twenty-five, Norbert looked the way their father once had. Thick black hair, bushy beard of the same colour, brown eyes and broad shoulders. The similarities ended with their looks. Where Ritter was even tempered and thoughtful, Norbert was quick to anger and easily offended. "Of course not. I just think I should get a chance to try too."

"You're only a child, what makes you think you can last the night?" Harriman asked.

Lenard hated the way Harriman always acted like he was so much older. Twenty-two only made Harriman four years older than him. Harriman was narrow framed, like himself, had a trimmed goatee, and like both he and Norbert had thick black hair and brown eyes. "I don't know that I can, but don't I deserve the chance to try?"

"Father's already made up his mind. Quit hounding him," Norbert said.

"I suppose it's only fair he should have his chance to try and catch the thief," Ritter said.

When Norbert and Harriman

started arguing with Ritter over his decision, Lenard decided it was time to slip away and get ready to catch the thief. Collecting his bow and arrows, he made his way to the Royal Gardens. Wandering along the paths, he admired his father's work. Ritter wouldn't survive without these gardens to take care of. Eventually Lenard reached the heart of the gardens and the apple tree that grew there.

The tree bore golden apples, which were counted every day. For the last three mornings the king had found another apple missing. As head gardener, it was his father's job to maintain, care for and protect the gardens. Including the apple tree. For the past two nights his brothers had been trying to catch the thief, but both had fallen asleep at midnight.

Lenard looked around the area, trying to decide where he should wait for the thief. He discarded the shrubs his brothers had hidden in, deciding to wait under the tree. Maybe seeing someone might scare the thief off. It was more important to stop them from stealing the apples than it was to catch them. He couldn't afford to fail. Not only was his father's job on the line, but his brothers were likely to torment him for years if he did. Although he doubted they'd be any happier with him if he succeeded where they'd failed.

He settled in under the tree, leaning against the rough bark. He kept his bow across his lap and had an arrow ready in case the thief showed his face. Late afternoon slowly became night and coloured lanterns were lit by his father's assistants. They didn't dispel all the shadows and there were plenty of spaces where a thief could hide. As the night grew later, he began to wish he'd thought to bring something to eat. In the distance he heard the clock tower strike nine. There were still hours yet to get through. He stifled a yawn. A noise caught his attention and he looked in that direction.

Ritter walked towards him carrying a cloth wrapped bundle. He held it out. "I thought you might be hungry."

"Thanks." Lenard opened the cloth to find bread and cheese. "I forgot to bring something to eat."

"Are you sure you'll be fine? The days and nights are getting cooler now."

"I'm fine." He hated how his father treated him like he was still the same sickly child he'd once been. "You don't have to worry about me."

"Should I have brought you a blanket?"

Lenard shook his head. "The cool air will help me stay awake. Go to bed, Father."

Ritter hesitated. "Are you sure you'll be fine?"

"Yes, now go to bed. And quit worrying."

Ritter stared at him a moment longer before he turned and walked away.

Lenard watched his father go. When had Ritter started to grow old? It didn't seem possible, but it was like he'd aged overnight. Was the theft of the golden apples affecting him that much? He sat up straighter, more determined than ever to stay awake and catch the thief.

Once his food was finished, Lenard struggled to remain awake. The clock striking eleven startled him and he feared he must have drifted off at some stage because he couldn't remember hearing it strike ten. He took a deep breath, trying to remain alert. It was an effort and several times he found himself drifting off. When the clock struck twelve, he heard a rustling in the apple tree. Peering upwards, he saw a gold coloured bird trying to steal one of the golden apples. Lenard leapt to his feet, firing an arrow at the bird. It darted away, the arrow knocking a tail feather from it before it flew off into the night. Disappointed he'd missed, Lenard collected the feather and was surprised to find it was solid gold.

He spent the rest of the night pacing around the tree in case the bird returned, worried that if he remained seated he might fall asleep. In the morning his father and brothers came to check on him and he showed them the feather, telling them about the bird.

Norbert took the feather from him and examined it. "I knew it couldn't be anything natural or we wouldn't have fallen asleep."

Lenard was tempted to point out that he hadn't fallen asleep, but didn't want to start an argument with his brother first thing in the morning. "What are we going to do about the bird? What if it keeps coming back for more apples?"

Ritter took the feather from Norbert, turning it in his hands as he looked at it. "We need to tell the king."

King Alfred and his advisers spent

the morning debating the meaning of the golden bird, finally coming to the conclusion that it was something the king must have. Norbert convinced the king to let him try and find the bird since it was his family who'd discovered its existence. Lenard tried to point out that he'd been the one to discover it, but no one paid him any attention. Frustration filled him. It was bad enough his brothers treated him like a child without others doing the same. Swallowing his disappointment, he helped his brother pack for the journey and stood beside Ritter and Harriman as they watched Norbert leave.

When several weeks passed and Norbert hadn't returned, Harriman convinced Ritter to let him go. He pointed out how it probably wouldn't be a good idea to tell the king they'd failed after having convinced him they could succeed. After more weeks passed, and Harriman failed to return, Lenard tried to convince his father to let him go after the bird.

"You would have me lose all my sons?"

"I know I can find the bird. I was the one who discovered it."

"You've never been far from home, how could you undertake a journey such as this?"

"Please, Father. Don't I deserve a chance to try too? And what would you tell the king if we didn't do everything possible to find the bird before admitting failure?"

"I would rather face a thousand angry kings than to lose you too."

It took hours, but Lenard eventually convinced Ritter to let him go. He set out the next day with far more money than his father could spare, food wrapped up in a cloth, his bow and arrows and his father's pleas to take care and return home safely.

After travelling half the day he came to a forest. He hadn't gone far into it before he saw a large fox. Larger than any fox he'd ever seen. Fitting an arrow to his bow he took aim, thinking it better to kill the beast before it saw him and attacked.

The fox looked directly at him. "Don't shoot me and I'll give you some advice to help you on your quest. I know you've been sent to fetch the golden bird for your king."

Startled, Lenard lowered his bow. "How do you know?"

"Everyone knows your king wants to have the golden bird for his own. There's no other reason for someone from your town to travel along this road. Besides, the other two men who came this way told the people in the next village about the important quest they were on.

"Did you speak to them too?" Lenard guessed the fox was talking about his brothers.

"I gave them the same advice I've offered to tell you, but they ignored it. Do you want to hear the advice?"

That sounded like his brothers. He inclined his head. "I'll listen to your advice." That didn't mean he had to take it.

"Follow this road to the next village where you'll want to stay the night as the roads hereabout are too dangerous to travel after dark. When you come into the village you'll see two inns. One is pleasant and beautiful to look at. Don't stay there.

Stay in the other one, even though it looks poor and mean."

He could understand why neither of his brothers would have taken that advice. They'd probably thought the fox had been playing a trick on them. He guessed it wouldn't hurt to stay in the inn the fox had suggested. "Thank you." Lenard started to continue along the road.

"Since you didn't shoot at me like the other men did, sit upon my tail and I'll take you to the village."

Lenard eyed the fox. The creature seemed large enough to be able to carry his weight. "Thank you. I would appreciate that." He climbed upon the fox's tail and the creature took off. They went so quickly the wind whistled past them and they were soon at the village, well before the day ended.

Lenard climbed off the fox and, thanking him, went into the inn the fox had told him to use. Even though it didn't look the best, the food was filling and the place was clean. After an uneventful night he set out on his journey again. He hadn't gone far before he came across the fox.

"I see you took my advice," the fox said.

"Thank you for your suggestion. I passed a quiet evening there."

"Let me offer you some more advice."

"Certainly." Lenard guessed it couldn't hurt to listen to the fox again.

"If you wish to find the golden bird, go straight ahead until you come to a castle before which lies an entire troop of soldiers fast asleep and snoring. Take no notice of them. Go into the castle and look for a room where the golden bird sits in a wooden cage. Beside it stands a beautiful golden cage. Whatever you do, don't try to take the bird from the wooden cage and put it into the golden one."

"Thank you." That sounded simple enough. Lenard started to walk away.

The fox stretched out his tail. "Would you like me to take you there?"

"I'd appreciate that." Lenard clambered onto the fox and they took off down the road. Again they went fast enough that the wind whistled through Lenard's hair.

The fox stopped at the castle gate. "Don't forget what I told you."

The moment Lenard clambered off the fox, it headed back along the road they'd travelled. He faced the castle with the troop of soldiers asleep before it. Taking care not to wake any of them, Lenard made his way to the castle door and went inside. He wandered through the many rooms until he found the golden bird.

It sat quietly in its wooden cage. The three golden apples it had stolen were nearby. He crossed the room and reached for the cage. His hand remained poised above it as he eyed the flimsy item. He had a long journey ahead of him. He couldn't go anywhere near the speed the fox had travelled. Would the cage handle the rigours of a journey? His gaze was drawn to the gold cage nearby. It looked far more suitable for a long journey and he wouldn't risk losing the bird after having found it. He couldn't see a single reason why the fox would have suggested taking the wooden cage. Besides, how could he present the golden bird to King Alfred in something so shabby?

Opening the door of the wooden cage, Lenard reached in and took hold of the bird. It squawked noisily, struggling to escape his grip. The sound woke the soldiers who came running to see what was happening.

"Return the bird to its cage," one of the soldiers ordered.

Seeing drawn swords, Lenard returned the bird, wishing he'd listened to the fox. As soon as the birdcage was closed, the soldiers marched him to the king. He didn't have a chance to say anything before the king was sending him to the dungeons where he was to be held until he could appear before the court the next morning. Not that he had much to say in his defence. He didn't think the king would let him go because King Alfred wanted the golden bird.

Lenard slept fitfully, dreading facing the court. When he finally did, he was sentenced to hang. "Isn't there anything I can do for you in exchange for my life?"

The king waved the soldiers away from him before they could lead him from the room. "There is one thing I desire. It's the golden horse that runs as swiftly as the wind."

"I've heard of that horse." Lenard tried to sound sincere, nodding slowly like he'd seen the old men do when they imparted their knowledge. He had no idea where he could find the horse, but he hadn't known where to find the golden bird and he'd managed to track it down. "Set me free and I'll bring it to you in exchange for the golden bird."

"Very well. If you bring the golden horse here, the golden bird and your life are yours. If you don't bring him here within a reasonable amount of time I'll send my soldiers after you."

As soon as his gear was returned to him and he was released, Lenard left the castle behind, having no idea in which direction to travel. He was relieved when he saw his old friend the fox. "Have you heard of the golden horse that runs as swiftly as the wind?"

"I have. If I tell you, will you listen to my advice this time?"

"Yes, I'm sorry I didn't listen to you." Lenard barely managed not to point out that it would have been helpful if the fox had told him why he should have left the bird in the flimsy wooden cage.

The fox stared at him for nearly a minute before he spoke. "If you promise to follow my advice I'll take you to the horse. There's a castle that lies in that direction." The fox momentarily turned his head in the correct direction before he again looked at Lenard. "The golden horse stands in his stall, his groom asleep nearby. Put the leather saddle on him and lead him out of his stall. Whatever you do, don't use the golden saddle."

Relieved the fox was still willing to help him, Lenard nodded. "Certainly. I can do that."

"Hop on and I'll take you there."

Lenard clambered onto the fox and they were soon racing towards his destination. Like the last two times, they went fast enough the wind whistled past them. The fox didn't slow until they reached the next castle. As soon as the fox came to a stop, Lenard climbed off and thanked him. He watched as the fox disappeared into the nearby forest. Taking a deep breath, he turned to face the castle. The task seemed simple enough. Find the stables, put the saddle on the horse and get out of there. If the horse was as swift as the king had said, he'd be back before the day was over.

It didn't take him long to find the stables. They were massive, with rows upon rows of horses. He eventually found the golden horse at the far end of the stable. The groom was asleep nearby. He saw the two saddles and reached for the leather one. Examining it, he found it nearly worn through in places. Surely the fox didn't expect him to use a saddle that was likely to break. He began to wish the fox had joined him so he could have asked him what he should do. The fox wasn't here.

He had another look at the horse. The golden creature tossed his head and Lenard made up his mind. There was no way he'd even think about riding such a powerful beast and risk being thrown from him. A horse that could travel as fast as the wind might cross a country in a single day and he'd never be able to find him again. He turned from the leather saddle and picked up the golden one instead. Besides, a horse that magnificent deserved a saddle equally as beautiful. A glance at the groom showed he was still asleep and Lenard opened the door to the golden horse's stall.

"All right boy, let's do this." He kept his voice soft and soothing.

The moment the saddle touched the horse's back it reared into the air, whinnying so loudly it woke the groom. Spying Lenard in the stall, the groom called out, "Guards! Quick. There's a thief stealing the golden horse."

Lenard dropped the saddle, but there was no way for him to escape. The groom stood in front of the only exit, the sound of running feet warning the guards were on their way. Would the horse have made such a racket if he'd used the leather saddle? Why hadn't the fox told him?

When the guards arrived, they took him prisoner. The next morning they brought him before the court and he was soon sentenced to death.

He drew away from them when they tried to lead him away.

"Is there anything I can do in exchange for my life?"

The king whispered to his adviser before turning to Lenard. "Yes. The neighbouring kingdom has a princess who is far more beautiful than any other woman. Her father has rejected every suitor. If you bring Princess Della here, I will not only let you live, but I'll also give you the golden horse. Fail and my soldiers will hunt you down and kill you."

Lenard thought of the threat from the king who owned the golden bird. Somehow he had to figure this out. Surely convincing the neighbouring king to allow his daughter to marry this king couldn't be that difficult. It had to at least be simpler than stealing the golden bird or the golden horse. "I won't fail, Your Majesty."

Once the guards returned his gear and escorted him from the castle, Lenard set out towards the neighbouring kingdom. He hadn't gone far when the fox joined him. Relief poured through him at the sight of the creature.

"You didn't listen."

Relief evaporated as quickly as it had arrived. "I'm sorry. I thought the leather saddle might break. It was old and worn."

"You should have listened."

"I know. I'm sorry." He bit back the argument that the fox should have explained himself better. "I need your help fetching the princess of the neighbouring kingdom."

"Will you listen?"

"I will. I'll do exactly what you say."

"Are you certain? Twice now you've failed to follow my advice."

Lenard thought of the two kings who would send soldiers to end his life if he didn't fulfil their wishes. "Yes. Tell me how I can get the princess for the king." The fox stared at him long enough that Lenard began to think he wouldn't help.

"Every night at twelve o'clock the princess goes alone to the bathing house to wash. At other times of the day she's surrounded by guards, soldiers, servants, lords and ladies. If you should kiss her, she'll allow you to lead her away. But whatever you do, don't let her take leave of her parents."

"I can do that." It sounded easy enough.

"Hop on and I'll take you there."

Lenard clambered onto the fox, who raced through the countryside the moment he was seated. Again they went fast enough the wind whistled past them and shortly the fox arrived at an imposing castle.

As soon as Lenard climbed off him, the fox said, "Make sure you follow my advice."

"I will." He watched the fox disappear into the nearby forest. Remembering the instructions, he looked for the bathing house and hid himself to wait for midnight. The hours passed slowly and he wished he'd thought to ask the soldiers for some food for his journey. The meagre meal they'd served him last night in his cell hadn't done much to help his hunger. Nor had the similar meal the previous night in the other king's dungeon.

When Della finally entered the bathing house, Lenard remained frozen in place for several minutes. He'd never seen anyone so beautiful before in his life. Stumbling out of his hiding place his face reddened when she looked his way. "Your Royal Highness." He bowed.

"Who are you and how did you get in here?"

Remembering the fox's advice, Lenard crossed the space between them and kissed the princess. Drawing away from her, he gazed into her eyes trying to remember what he was meant to say. "Will you leave your home and come away with me?"

Della smiled up at him. "Ever since my brother Wilford was lost to us, my father has kept me a prisoner for fear something would happen to me. Yes, I'll go with you."

Lenard felt his face heat again and he started to explain she wouldn't exactly be going with him. That he'd promised to take her to the neighbouring king. Before he had the chance, Della spoke again.

"Let me say goodbye to my parents and pack a few things."

Reminding himself of the fox's advice, Lenard shook his head. "We don't have time for that. We must leave immediately."

Della begged and pleaded. When tears formed in her eyes Lenard finally gave in. He walked beside her to the castle, dreading the moment when she'd say goodbye to her parents. He still couldn't believe he'd actually given in and agreed. What had he been thinking? He looked towards her, about to say he'd changed his mind. He was too late. Soldiers came forward and surrounded them, dragging him before the king who'd been woken from his slumber.

Lenard knelt before the king, trying to remain calm. "Your Majesty."

The king glared at him, still dressed in his nightclothes. "You would steal my daughter away from me?"

"I can expl-"

"I will let you have her on one condition."

Lenard's jaw dropped open. He stared at the king for a moment. "You will?"

The king inclined his head. "Yes." His lips twisted into a smile.

The mocking expression made

Lenard want to run from the castle. Instead, he straightened his shoulders and met the king's gaze. "How can I be of service, Your Majesty?"

The king's mocking smile remained in place. "I want you to dig away the hill that is in the way of the view from my window. You have eight days to complete this task. If you fail, I will end your life."

Lenard rose to his feet. "Have someone show me where the hill is and it will be done, Your Majesty."

The king laughed, waving one of his soldiers forward. "Show him."

Lenard followed a soldier from the room, unable to resist looking towards Della one last time. She mouthed some words at him and he could have sworn she was telling him good luck. His spirits lightened considerably and he followed the soldier out of the castle. When he reached the hill his spirits plummeted again. Surely the king had set him an impossible task. The hill looked more like a mountain.

He took the shovel the soldier handed him and watched as the man strode away, leaving him alone at the foot of the hill. Believing the task was completely impossible, Lenard began to dig. What else could he do? For seven days he dug, his hands blistering and his muscles protesting at the continual, strenuous work. The only breaks he took were to eat the three meals a servant brought him every day and to sleep a couple of hours each evening.

Tired and exhausted, he leaned against the shovel as he struggled to keep his eyes open. He didn't have time to sleep. Tomorrow was the last day he had to clear the hill. Even though it seemed like he'd done very little, he couldn't bring himself to give up.

The fox trotted up and stopped beside him. "You didn't follow my advice, did you?"

"No." He was too exhausted to explain himself or even apologise.

"Lie down and sleep. I'll help you tonight."

"Why?"

"Because you've treated me well. All others have attacked me, even when I've asked them to leave me be. None of them believe I mean no harm." The fox opened his mouth in what could almost have been called a smile, showing sharp teeth. "If only you didn't have such an annoying tendency not to follow advice."

"I've always planned to, but then

other options start to look more logical." He thought of Della and his illogical decision to let her say goodbye to her parents. "Or a beautiful princess begs and pleads until I give in." He smiled wryly.

The fox inclined his head, making a sharp sound that might have been a laugh. "Go to sleep, Lenard. You're nearly falling asleep where you stand. I'll work for you tonight."

"Thank you." He stumbled away from the hill and curled up in a sheltered hollow where he'd slept each night the past week. It didn't take him long to fall into an exhausted and dreamless sleep.

When Lenard was woken the next morning by the rising sun, he reluctantly staggered to his feet. He stared at where the hill should have been and found only flat ground.

Taking a few hesitant steps forward, he rubbed at his eyes, unable to believe what he saw. The hill was gone and the fox was nowhere in sight. He ran forward, slowly turning on the spot where it had once risen. The ground was flat and even, stretching off into the distance. A grin formed and Lenard nearly shouted in relief. Not knowing who might be watching him, he contained his exuberance and strode towards the castle.

The soldiers escorted him to the king, where he sat in the throne room, lords and ladies gathered around him. Lenard's gaze was momentarily drawn to Della as he reached the king. He wondered what she thought about her father's decree. He bowed deeply to the king. "Your Majesty."

"I was informed you've completed the task I set you and saw with my own eyes that the hill has been removed."

"Yes, Your Majesty." He tried to gauge how the king felt about that fact, but his expression was neutral.

"Never let it be said that I am not a man of my word." The king held out his hand towards his daughter as he rose from his throne. "Della."

She crossed to his side, taking his hand. "Yes, Father."

The king held out his daughter's hand to Lenard. "You are to go with this young man."

Lenard took Della's hand, bowing over it. "I am honoured, Your Royal Highness."

Della smiled at him. "I have said my goodbyes and am ready to leave whenever you are."

Continuing to hold her hand, Lenard walked beside her, taking her past the castle gates. He looked in the direction they had to travel, not sure how to break the news that he was taking her to the neighbouring king. The last thing he wanted to do was to give her to the king with the golden horse, but what else could he do? If he didn't deliver the princess, the king's soldiers would hunt him down and kill him.

As they stepped into the forest, Della turned to him and asked, "Where are we going?"

The fox stepped out from amongst the trees, stopping on the path in front of them, causing Della to gasp. "Haven't you told her yet?"

Lenard shook his head. It hardly seemed right for him to say he'd been busy trying to think of a way out of his task.

"Told me what?" Della looked from one to the other. "And who is he?" She nodded towards the fox.

"A friend." He really didn't want to answer the first question she'd asked.

"How would you like to have all three?" the fox asked.

Lenard didn't hesitate. "Tell me how."

"What is going on?" Della demanded.

It was the moment he'd been dreading. He couldn't put it off any longer. "I was supposed to deliver you to the neighbouring king in exchange for him letting me live." He thought it best not to say there'd also been a golden horse involved. At least not yet.

Della drew away from him. "You

did all that for some other man? When I watched you from my balcony, I thought you laboured for my hand. Now you tell me it was all for someone else."

He almost groaned. This wasn't how he'd expected the moment to go. "The moment I set eyes on you, I regretted that I'd have to leave you with another man."

"You did?" Even though the anger left Della's voice, she still sounded suspicious.

Lenard nodded. "Yes. If he hadn't threatened to kill me if I didn't bring you to him I never would have considered taking you there."

"Why not leave the country? We could travel so far away that he'd never find us," Della said.

"If only it was that simple." He told her about the golden bird he'd discovered stealing King Alfred's apples. About how his brothers had gone in search of it and his father had reluctantly let him go when they hadn't returned. He spoke about how he couldn't desert his father like that, no matter how much he wished he could, for her sake.

The fox remained quiet throughout Lenard's story. Only Della occasionally interrupted with questions. When he finished speaking, she reached for his hands, clasping them in her own.

"You are right, it isn't that simple. You can't desert your poor father." Her expression clouded. "I once knew someone who was worth sacrificing my own happiness for theirs."

Lenard feared it was a suitor that

Della loved and hadn't been allowed to marry. "Who?"

"Wilford. Not a day goes by that I don't miss my brother and wish I knew how he died and where his remains lay."

"I'm sorry."

"Thank you." Still holding Lenard's hands, Della turned to the fox. "What do you suggest we do?"

"That depends on whether Lenard is willing to follow my advice this time."

He thought back to every time his journey had gone well. The uneventful night at the inn and going to sleep, leaving the fox to level the hill. "No matter what happens, I'll follow your advice." His gaze left the fox and fell on Della. "I have too much to lose this time."

The fox made a sound that could

have been a laugh. "And your life wasn't too much to lose?"

Lenard reluctantly smiled. "Obviously not."

"We shall see. Now listen carefully. When you see the king, show him Princess Della and ask him to fetch the golden horse. When he has done so, remind him you have brought the princess to him as he requested. Make sure he admits you've completed the task he set and you owe him nothing. All he asked of you was to bring the princess to him. Understand?"

Lenard nodded. "How will that help? I don't want to leave Princess Della with him."

"I don't want to stay with him," Della protested. "You can't imagine how relieved I was when my father turned down his marriage offer."

"Do you understand so far?" The

fox used an exaggerated tone of patience.

"Yes." Lenard and Della spoke together.

"Once he agrees, mount the golden horse and take your leave of everyone, leaning down to shake their hands. Shake Princess Della's hand last, swing her up behind you and gallop away. I'll meet you at the door of the castle where the golden bird lives."

Della grinned. "How clever." She turned to Lenard. "What do you think?"

He slowly nodded, trying not to think about all the things that could go wrong. Look what had happened the last time he'd tried to take the golden horse. He couldn't come up with a better plan. "I'm ready to give it a try."

"Then both of you hop on and I'll take you to the castle," the fox said.

Lenard clambered onto the fox and helped Della sit behind him, her hands clutching him tightly, the bow and quiver slung at his back preventing her from being as close to him as he'd like. This had to work, he couldn't stand the thought of leaving her behind. The fox took off and Lenard clung to his fur as the wind whistled past them. In no time at all they reached the castle and both climbed down.

Della was grinning. "I have never travelled so fast in my entire life. That was so much fun."

Lenard couldn't help returning her grin, even though he worried about what was about to happen. He held out his hand. "Shall we see if the horse is as fast as the fox?" He was pretty certain he'd managed to keep his worries from his voice.

Della slipped her hand in his. "Oh, absolutely. I look forward to it."

Lenard kept hold of her hand as they walked through the castle gates. The soldiers didn't detain him and some even stared at them with mouths gaping, a couple hastily bowing. When they reached the front door, two soldiers escorted them to the king who was in the stable courtyard. Lenard sent a nervous glance towards the stables, remembering how the horse had behaved when he'd tried to saddle it.

Still holding Della's hand, he bowed. "Your Majesty."

The king's eyes remained on Della. "You are as beautiful as I remember."

Della curtsied, smiling at the king. "Thank you, Your Majesty.

Lenard released her hand, gesturing for her to go to the king's side. "I've brought Princess Della as requested. Can you bring me the golden horse, saddled and ready to go?"

"Yes, yes, of course." The king waved one of his soldiers forward. "Have the groom ready the horse."

When the king started to turn away, Lenard feared he'd leave the courtyard before the horse could be brought out. "You're happy I've completed the task you set, Your Majesty? That of bringing Princess Della here."

"Yes, yes. I thought I'd already agreed you had."

"And you have no reason to send your soldiers after me since the task is now complete?" Lenard glanced towards the stables. What was taking the groom so long?

"No need at all." The king sounded annoyed. He turned to Della. "Let me show you your new home."

Lenard saw the look of panic that flittered across her face, quickly replaced by a smile. He took a step closer to them. "I haven't had a chance to bid you both farewell."

"Nor have I had the chance to thank you for bringing me here," Della said.

"Well, get it over with," the king said impatiently.

The groom brought the golden horse out of the stable and Lenard nearly cheered. Instead he took the reins and swung up into the worn, leather saddle. With a shallow nod in thanks to the groom, he turned to the king. "Thank you for keeping your word, Your Majesty." He nudged the horse into a walk and stopped in front of the king, holding out his hand for the man to shake it.

The king stared disdainfully at the hand held out, looking like he might refuse. "A king always keeps his word." The handshake was extremely brief.

Lenard held out his hand to Della. "I hope you'll be happy, Your Royal Highness."

Della took his hand, grinning. "I plan to be."

Lenard swung her up behind him and urged the golden horse into a gallop. The shouts of the king and soldiers were quickly left behind as he guided the horse to the next castle, half amazed that everything had gone as planned. Della was seated behind him, holding onto him tightly, the bow and quiver at his back preventing her from leaning in close, the golden horse crossing the countryside as fast as the wind. Now if only things went as well with the golden bird.

Reaching the next castle, both of them dismounted, finding the fox waiting for them not far from the castle gates. Lenard glanced towards the soldiers at the gate, all of them looking like they were asleep with how they leaned against the walls.

"That was a marvellous ride. Far better than riding on the fox." Della turned to the fox with a grin. "No offence to you, but it's far more comfortable to ride a horse."

The fox nodded once. "None taken."

"What's the next plan?" Lenard asked.

"I'm glad to see you finally followed my advice."

Lenard smiled. "It wasn't the first time. The inn was comfortable even if it wasn't in the finest state."

The fox nodded once more. "Princess Della will remain out here with me while you go to the castle and ask the king to bring you the golden bird. Tell him you wish to be certain it's the real bird. Make sure you have him agree that you've completed the task and brought the golden horse to him like he requested. Whatever you do, don't get off the horse. As soon as you have the bird, gallop outside to where the princess and I will be waiting. Don't stop for either of us. I'll carry the princess and we'll stop far from here before you take her upon your horse."

Lenard turned to Della. "Does this sound fine to you?"

"I would have enjoyed going in there to see what happens, but it's probably for the best that I don't. How would you explain my presence? You can tell me what happens later."

"Of course, Princess Della."

Della laughed. "Surely you can call me Della. After all, not only have you stolen a kiss from me, but we're also sharing an adventure."

He felt his face redden, the heat increasing when Della laughed again. Not knowing what to say to her, he nodded in answer and turned to the fox. "I'm ready."

"Make sure you follow my advice."

"I will."

"Even though there isn't as much at risk this time?" Della asked.

Lenard took in the sight of her, his gaze stopping on her face. How could he expect her to want to continue travelling with him if he didn't have transport for her? He doubted the fox would carry Della all the way home for him. Surely he'd leave eventually. "There's still much at risk." He closed the distance between them, taking Della's hand. "I'll return as soon as possible."

Della leaned in, kissing him.

Lenard released her hand, wrapping his arms around her. The kiss ended far too soon and he stared down at her, wanting to draw her back for another one. Instead he let her go when she pulled away from him.

A smile slowly formed as Della took another step away from him, stopping at the fox's side. "Don't keep me waiting too long."

He stumbled as he backed away. "I won't." He swung up into the saddle.

"Remember my advice," the fox said.

With a nod, Lenard rode towards the castle, remaining on the horse. Reaching the front door, he called out to a soldier. "Tell your king I've brought the golden horse and I'm waiting here to show him."

The soldier hurried away and Lenard waited impatiently, trying not to keep glancing over his shoulder to catch a glimpse of Della and the fox. It was impossible to see either of them from where he waited.

The king came out to stand on the steps. "I hardly believed my ears when the solider told me you had the golden horse." He turned to the soldier who'd fetched him. "Bring the golden bird." He waved another soldier forward. "Take the horse to the stable."

"One moment." Lenard made the horse move back away from the soldier's hand. "Do you agree I completed the task you set me? That of bringing the golden horse here."

"Certainly. And you shall have your life and the golden bird in exchange for your efforts. Now dismount and allow my man to take the horse to the stables."

"I haven't seen the golden bird as yet," Lenard said.

"Are you saying you doubt I'll keep my word?" The king's tone was indignant and his eyes narrowed. "How dare you suggest such a thing? I'm a man of my word."

Lenard was relieved to see the

soldier step outside with the caged bird. "I'm sure you are, I want to make sure your staff are equally honourable. Please let me see if that is the true golden bird."

The king waved the soldier forward, his gaze remaining narrowed and his lips thinned in anger.

Lenard took the wooden cage and peered in at the bird. It was the same bird he'd fired his bow at so long ago. "As you said, you're a man of your word." With a nod to the king, Lenard urged his horse to race for the castle gates. Behind him he heard the king roar. Ahead he saw Della seated upon the fox, the two of them heading for the forest. He followed behind, unable to catch them. Eventually the fox came to a stop in the forest not far from the village where he'd spent his first night of the journey. He could see glimpses of it through the trees.

Lenard dismounted, grinning when Della threw herself at him, kissing him once more. This time he had only one arm to wrap around her and he was tempted to place the cage on the ground so he could hold her like he had before. The kiss was ended before he had a chance.

"This is the bird that started it all?" Della peered into the cage.

Lenard nodded.

"He's so beautiful." She took the cage from him. Her eyes widened. "And far heavier than I would have thought. I'm surprised he can fly."

"Come speak with me a moment, Lenard," the fox said.

Lenard looked between the fox and Della.

She waved him away. "I'll be fine."

Lenard walked beside the fox, sending frequent glances towards Della who was whistling at the bird, trying to get it to sing. "Was there something you wanted?"

"Yes." The fox stopped and met Lenard's gaze. "Have you not gained all you sought and more?"

"I have. Thank you for helping me. I like to think we've become friends." He couldn't have managed without the fox's advice and help. Again he glanced towards Della.

"Then please grant me a favour of my own."

"How can I help you?"

"I beg you to kill me and cut off my head and feet."

"No!" Lenard took a stumbling step away from the fox. "I couldn't. How could you ask that of me? Why would you ask that of me? Ask something else and I'll do it, but not that."

"Please. That is all I require of you."

"I'm sorry, I can't do it. You're asking me to kill a friend."

The fox lowered his head. "I didn't think you'd be able to. You have too kind a heart, but I had to try."

"I'm sorry." He wished he could oblige the fox, but even the thought of hurting the creature had him shaking his head. "I'm sorry."

"Even though you've refused to do me this favour, I'll advise you one more time. Ransom no one from the gallows and sit beside no river. Do this and you'll arrive home safely."

That sounded simple enough. Why would he wish to pay to have a criminal escape a hanging? And there were plenty of other places to rest than beside a river. "Thank you. If there's ever anything else I can do for you, please ask."

"Take care, Lenard." The fox turned and disappeared into the forest.

Della came to stand beside him, carrying the cage. "I didn't get a chance to say goodbye. What did he want?"

"A favour." Maybe he'd be able to tell her later, but not now. "We're not far from my home. We should be there before nightfall." He took the cage from her.

"I can't wait to meet your father."

Lenard mounted the horse and helped Della sit behind him. "I can't wait to introduce you to him." He kept the horse at a walk, not wanting to scare the villagers by galloping through there at the speed of the wind.

As they passed through the village, he heard an uproar coming from the centre. He stopped to talk to a gentleman. "What's going on?"

It took the gentlemen a moment to get over his surprise at Lenard's companions. "Two men are about to be hung. Brothers who turned to robbery."

Lenard continued through the village, the road taking him past the crowd. He came to a stop when he saw the two men standing on the gallows. It was his brothers. There was no way he could travel on and leave them to their fate.

Dismounting, Lenard handed the cage to Della and asked her to wait. He wound his way through the crowd and mounted the stairs to the gallows platform. "Can't these men be saved? Surely there must be something I can do so I won't need to take back the news of their death to their aged father."

The man who stood on the platform near Lenard's brothers shook his head. "They've had their chances. We've pardoned them several times and still they've returned to their thieving ways."

A woman called out from the crowd. "Make him pay back all they've stolen." A murmur went through the crowd.

"What would it cost to ransom them?" As he spoke the words Lenard couldn't help thinking that if the fox had known it was his brothers who were about to be hung, he never would have given him such advice.

It took nearly twenty minutes for the village to come to an agreement. Lenard handed over all the money he had left from what his father had given him for his journey, relieved he'd needed to spend so little of it previously. There wasn't enough and he was forced to give his bow and arrows to pay the balance. His brothers were released into his custody and he headed towards Della.

When she rode out of the village, he trailed behind her, thinking it was probably best. The village people might change their minds and ask for more money to cover his brothers' ransom.

"Is that the bird?" Norbert gestured to the cage Della still held.

"Yes."

"Who's the woman on the golden horse? Why has she got the bird?" Harriman asked.

Lenard thought of everything that had happened. From what the fox had said, both his brothers had been given the chance to follow his advice. Neither had taken it and both had tried to kill him. Pointing this out probably wouldn't be a good idea. "She's travelling with me to give the golden bird to King Alfred."

"I bet you think you're better than us now," Norbert sneered.

He tried not to sigh, but it was a close call. "No, I was lucky to have had help." Help they'd rejected. He wondered if he should call out to Della to stop, mount the horse and ride away to leave his brothers to find their own way home. When he thought about how he'd have to explain that to his father, he decided he could put up with their company a little longer.

"What help?" Harriman demanded.

Again a sigh nearly escaped. Did

they have to keep questioning him? "Princess Della gave me some help." He gestured towards her.

"Who else?" Harriman asked.

It was going to be a long trip home. He tried to think of a way to change the subject, but all that came to mind was asking his brothers where they'd been all this time. It probably wouldn't be a good idea to ask them. "Are you both well? Unharmed?"

"Now it comes," Norbert said. "I suppose you're going to expect us to shower you with gratitude."

This time the sigh did escape. "I was only asking if you're well. The crowd back there didn't look too friendly."

"They were the thieves," Norbert snarled. "Their inn was enchanted and we lost all memory of our task."

"They encouraged us to remain, running up the bill so we were forced to steal to pay it," Harriman said.

Lenard guessed it wouldn't be a good idea to point out that following the fox's advice would have saved them that grief. "I'll see if I can get us home quicker." He hurried forward. "Princess Della. Wait up."

She stopped the horse and looked at him over her shoulder.

Reaching her, he mounted the horse, sitting behind her. "I'll be back in a few minutes to collect you." Not waiting for his brothers to reply, he urged the horse into a gallop and they flew through the forest. It didn't take long for him to reach the place where he'd first met the fox. He drew the horse to a stop and dismounted, taking the cage from Della so she could get off the horse too.

He returned the cage to her. "I won't be long."

"What happened to calling me Della?"

"It didn't seem appropriate in front of my brothers."

"Why not?"

He shrugged. When she continued to stare at him, he supposed he had to give her an answer. "I didn't think they should call you Della."

Della grinned. "I'll see you soon."

Lenard swung up into the saddle and turned the horse in the direction they'd come from. It didn't take long for the horse to reach Norbert and Harriman, who were arguing. He held out his hand to Harriman. "I'll give you a lift to where I left the princess."

Norbert hit Harriman's hand away when he reached for Lenard. "Why should you take him first? I'm the oldest."

Lenard bit back the words he knew were a bad idea to say out loud. Norbert was the last person he'd want to leave alone with Della. Harriman was the least argumentative and aggressive out of the two of them. "I thought you would be the one least likely to be attacked if robbers should come this way while I was gone."

"Are you saying I don't look like I can take care of myself?" Harriman asked.

"No, of course not." Lenard struggled to think of a way to prevent a fight.

"Maybe you should be the one to wait here while we go ahead," Norbert said. "I'll drop Harriman off and come back for you."

"No." He answered far too quickly

if the look his brothers shared was anything to judge by.

"Why not?" Harriman asked.

He avoided the question. "We can't leave Princess Della by herself all day. What if robbers should find her?"

"We could easily pull you off that horse," Norbert said.

"It's my horse." He regretted the words the moment he spoke them.

"I thought it belonged to the princess," Harriman said.

"Is she yours too?" Norbert asked.

Fleetingly he regretted not following the fox's advice. He pushed that feeling away. "Do you want a lift or do I leave you here?" He held his hand out to Harriman again.

"You wouldn't." Norbert lunged for the bridle.

The horse danced out of the way.

Lenard continued to hold out his hand. "Last chance."

Harriman took his hand and swung up behind him. "I'm not walking all that way home."

When Norbert lunged for the horse again, Lenard galloped away. He was relieved to find Della safely where he'd left her. Once Harriman had dismounted, Lenard turned his horse back in the direction he'd come from. "I won't be long."

"That's what you said last time. Do you think I'm going to believe you this time?"

Lenard grinned at the merriment in her eyes. "Yes." He took off before she could reply, reaching Norbert far too soon. Eventually there was going to be a fight. Norbert didn't look happy. He held out his hand. "Are you ready?"

Without a word, Norbert took his hand and swung up behind him. They returned to where Lenard had left Della and Harriman. He couldn't see them anywhere. Panic struck and he feared for her life. The sound of laughter drifted to him and he rode towards it, seeing Della picking berries from a bush near the edge of a river.

Spying them, she waved him over. "Come and join us. They're unbelievably sweet."

Giddy with relief, he was unable to reply. When he reached her side, he waited for Norbert to dismount so he could.

"Try one." Smiling, she held out a berry to him.

He took the offering, popping it in his mouth.

Della looked over his shoulder. "I

don't think much of your brothers." She kept her voice low.

Lenard glanced over his shoulder and saw his brothers had walked away and were standing on the riverbank, talking. "Sadly I've never really gotten along with them." He'd always thought it was because he'd been a sickly child and not been able to keep up with them.

"I'm not surprised. I don't think many people would." Della picked another handful of berries. "Come and join me and I'll share them with you." She walked towards the riverbank, glancing back at him with a smile.

He followed, tying the horse up to a tree before he joined her, sitting on the grassy banks. He took the berry she offered. "We'll have to leave soon. I'd like to return home before dark."

It was already late afternoon. Hopefully a horse as swift as the golden one would be able to manage, but it would take a few trips to get them all home. He didn't want to force the horse to carry too great a load.

Norbert strode towards them, Harriman following. "What do you plan to tell our father?"

Not liking the feeling it gave him to have Norbert towering over him, Lenard started to rise to his feet.

Norbert shoved him.

Della screamed.

Lenard fell over the steep bank, crashing into the shallow water below. Pain exploded through him. Ignoring it, he struggled to his feet.

"Leave me alone." Della screamed. There was a sharp sound of someone being slapped and she fell silent.

"Quiet. You will not say anything of this moment," Norbert warned.

Lenard tried to climb up the steep bank. Dirt and gravel shifted under his hands and feet and he slid to the ground. Pain exploded through him again and he wondered if he'd broken something.

"When we take you, the horse and the bird to King Alfred you'll tell him we won all three of you through our own labours," Norbert said.

"Why would I tell him that?" Della demanded.

"If you don't, we'll kill you," Harriman said. "Is that clear?"

"Yes." Della spat the word at him.

Lenard kept trying to climb the bank. It was impossible.

"Get on the horse," Norbert ordered.

"You can't expect the poor creature

to carry all three of us and the bird," Della said.

"I can and it will." Norbert's voice was firm. "Get on the horse now."

Lenard listened to them ride away and stopped struggling to climb the bank. He sat with his head in his hands and his knees drawn up, thinking about the fox's advice. Why hadn't he listened to him? He should have known by now that the fox always knew these things. What was he going to do?

No answer came to him and he continued to sit there as the sun set and the moon rose, his body aching from the fall. Eventually he drifted off to sleep, still trying to figure a way out of his predicament. Morning brought no answers. Unable to find a way to scale the steep banks, Lenard began to walk downstream. It didn't help. The bank continued to remain steep.

Several feet away a head peered over the top of the bank at him. "When will you learn to follow my advice?"

Lenard couldn't help grinning at the sight of his friend. "Hopefully soon."

"I hope so too. King Alfred is vexed. Princess Della won't stop crying nor tell anyone what her problem is. The golden horse refuses to eat and the golden bird won't sing. Your brothers have told your father you perished on your journey and they've set men to watch for you and kill you should you try to enter the town or castle."

He barely paid attention to what the fox said after hearing about Della.

"Is she hurt? Norbert and Harriman didn't harm her did they?"

"I tell you all that news, including there are men planning to kill you, and all you are worried about is Della's health? Have you no concern for yourself?"

"Of course, it's just…" His voice trailed off and he felt the heat rise in his face.

The fox made a strange sound.

Lenard stared up at him. "Are you laughing at me?"

"How can I leave you to perish down there when that is your first concern?" The fox drew back from the edge of the bank and his tail soon appeared, hanging down low. "Take hold of my tail and I'll pull you out of there."

Lenard grabbed hold of the fox's tail and with his help was able to scramble up the steep bank. He looked in the direction of home before facing the fox. "I don't suppose you have some advice for me."

"Will you follow it?"

"Yes. Without hesitation."

"There are some rags over there." The fox nodded to a shrub not far from them. "Put them on and I'll get you close to the castle. See King Alfred and tell him everything that has happened. He's a fair and just king and I know he'll listen to you."

Without questioning, Lenard changed into the ragged clothes, leaving his own beneath the shrub. He stared at them a moment. It seemed strange to have left home in well fitting clothes, with sufficient money, his bow and arrows and to have collected along the way a golden bird, a golden horse, and a beautiful princess only to be returning home in rags. He turned his back on the last of his possessions. "I'm ready."

"Hop on and I'll take you to the castle."

Lenard did as the fox told him and they were soon racing through the countryside, the wind whistling past them. When the fox eventually stopped, Lenard climbed off and listened as the fox told him how to reach the king without being discovered.

"Thank you, my friend. I hope one day to be able to repay you."

The fox inclined his head. "I hope you can too." He raced off, quickly disappearing from view.

Lenard stared after him for several minutes before he followed the fox's directions. It took him longer than he expected, but he eventually reached the throne room.

"What do you think you're doing in here, you filthy beggar?" One of the guards strode towards him.

He looked past the guard, raising his voice. "King Alfred, I'm Lenard, your gardener's youngest son. I have a tale you need to hear."

The king waved the guard aside. "Why are you dressed in rags?" He beckoned Lenard forward.

Lenard bowed. "My brothers sent men to kill me so I couldn't bring you news of their trickery, Your Majesty."

King Alfred turned to one of his footmen. "Bring a stool for the young man to sit on and something for him to drink. This sounds like it'll be a long tale and he looks wearied from his journey."

"Thank you, Your Majesty. I

appreciate your kindness." Lenard sat on the stool the footman brought him and took the cup held out by another, glad to rest his weary and aching body. When he was halfway through his tale, a servant burst into the throne room, another on his heels.

"The golden bird is singing, Your Majesty. I didn't come straight to you with the news for fear he'd stop again, but it doesn't look like he will," the first servant said.

"I have similar news," the second servant said. "The golden horse is eating and has stopped trying to escape from his stall."

King Alfred looked at Lenard thoughtfully. "One would think they were pleased to have you nearby. Now if only the princess would cease her weeping." His gaze left Lenard to fall on one of the footmen. "Fetch

Princess Della, maybe she'll cease her weeping and finally speak when she sees this young man." Once the footman had scurried away, the king indicated for Lenard to continue with his tale.

He was nearly finished when Della arrived. Seeing him, she raced across the room. He barely had time to rise to his feet before she reached him. "Lenard!" She threw her arms around him. "I was terrified they'd killed you. What happened?"

"We were about to learn," King Alfred said.

Della drew away from Lenard, dropping into a curtsey. "I beg your pardon, Your Majesty. I didn't mean to interrupt."

"That is fine, maybe now you'll have your own tale to tell."

Della stepped closer to Lenard, glancing around the room.

Lenard slid his arm around her waist. "I won't let them harm you. I was about to tell King Alfred about Norbert pushing me over the river bank."

"Please, continue with your story," King Alfred said.

Lenard remained standing, his arm around Della as he finished the story.

King Alfred turned to Della. "Do you disagree with anything Lenard said?"

"No. Or at least not about the things I witnessed. Norbert did push him over the bank and he and Harriman threatened to kill me if I didn't agree with their story."

"They shall be punished." King Alfred called guards to him. "Find them for me and the men they sent to kill Lenard." When the guards left, he addressed the rest of those in the throne room. "Everyone leave except Lenard and Princess Della."

Lenard's arm tightened at Della's waist. "Your Majesty, can I help you somehow?"

"No, I believe I can help you. It's obvious that the golden bird and golden horse shall never be mine. For some reason they think you're their master and fretted for your return. And I believe someone else fretted as well." King Alfred smiled at Della.

"Can you blame me?" Della asked.

"Certainly not. I have yet to meet a more honest, courageous and loyal man. I have no heir to lead this kingdom when I'm gone. I would like to make you my heir."

"Y… Your Majesty?" He stumbled over the words.

King Alfred chuckled. "Obviously we'll need to call a tailor, but what do you say?"

"I'm honoured, Your Majesty, but without the fox I wouldn't have accomplished anything."

"Then you've learned a very important lesson about ruling. Without good advisors, a king is nothing. So what do you say? Will you be my heir?"

"Of course he will." Della drew away from him and pushed him forward. "Go and thank the king properly."

Lenard stopped in front of the King and glanced towards Della. "I see what you mean, Your Majesty." He held out his hand. "Thank you. It would be an honour to be your heir."

King Alfred took his hand and shook it before embracing him, patting him heartily on the back. "I'll make it official tomorrow. In the meantime I'll have tailors prepare suitable clothes for you."

"If you don't mind, Your Majesty, I'd like to see my father and let him know I'm alive." He glanced towards Della again. "I'd also like to introduce him to Princess Della."

"Of course. I'll send the tailors to you there and tomorrow you can move into your own suite in the castle."

Lenard thanked the king again and took his leave. Holding Della's hand, he made his way to his father's home. The house was quiet, the front door open. Peering inside he saw his father sitting by the fire, staring sightlessly into the flames. He didn't look in the direction of the open door straight away, but when he finally did his eyes widened and he slowly rose to his feet.

Letting go of Della's hand, Lenard crossed the room to embrace his father. "I'm sorry I took so long to return home."

"They told me you were dead. I couldn't believe it when I heard. Why would they say that?"

"It's a very long tale, but first I want you to meet someone." He looked towards the doorway where Della stood and held out his hand. She joined him. "Father, meet Princess Della."

His father was full of questions and he started the story from the beginning, the moment he'd first encountered the fox. The tailors arrived partway through the story and he continued to speak as he was measured for new garments. They talked until late in the night and eventually Lenard ended the conversation to escort Della back to the castle. He was a while taking his leave of her and when he returned home his father had fallen asleep in the chair by the fire. Smiling, he draped a blanket over his father before making his way to his own bed.

* * *

Lenard had thought his first day back home was busy, but it was nothing compared to the following couple of weeks. After the official announcement that he was King Alfred's heir everyone wanted to meet him. There were dinner parties, balls and other events that he was expected to attend. He was relieved to have Della at his side since he wouldn't have known how to behave at such gatherings without her help.

Eventually he had to take a break from it all and he escaped into the forest for a walk by himself. It wasn't that he hated his new life. He actually enjoyed most of it, but there were times when it was nice to have a few minutes to himself. Or an hour or two.

A noise behind him had him turning, reaching for his new bow. He left it slung on his back when he saw it was his friend, the fox. "I've missed you. No one else gives me advice as good as yours."

"Does that mean you're ready to follow one more piece of advice?"

The smile that had formed when Lenard had first seen the fox, faded. He knew what his friend was about to say, but he couldn't help asking anyway. "How can I help you?"

"I beg you to listen to this advice far more carefully than any other I've ever given you. Please kill me and cut off my head and feet. How often have I given you bad advice?"

His heart sank. "Never. Are you sure you want me to do this?"

"More than anything else in the world."

Lenard drew his knife. He stared at the fox, who lay down at his feet. How could he bring himself to kill his friend? But how could he ignore his advice when every time he did something had gone wrong. Taking a deep breath, he followed the advice, blood coating both him and the ground.

Tears coursed down his face as he rose to his feet and stared at the fox, the head and feet lying separately. Why had the fox asked this of him? What was so terrible that the fox had sought his own death?

The body of the fox shuddered and something tried to escape from it. Lenard started to step away, but instead went forward and cut into the skin of the fox. A man emerged, his fine clothes coated in blood.

The man grinned. "About time you learned to listen to my advice."

Lenard laughed. "I told you it would be soon."

The man held out his hand. "Thank you, Lenard."

Lenard shook his hand. "What do I call you? I can't keep calling you fox."

The man chuckled. "Wilford."

Lenard frowned. Surely not. "Della's Wilford?"

"Yes. Thank you for releasing me

from this curse and for rescuing my sister."

"If I'd listened to you when I was in the castle where the golden bird once lived, I never would have rescued your sister."

Wilford grinned. "I didn't think you'd listen at the first two castles. I was pretty certain you wouldn't. But I had thought you might listen at the third castle."

"You wanted me to give your sister to the king that owned the golden horse?"

"No, I'd always planned to tell you how to escape with all three. The first day we met I knew you were worthy of my sister. You wouldn't cage her like my father did. Ready for some more advice?"

Lenard chuckled. "Always, my friend."

"My sister will appreciate knowing I'm still alive. Will you follow my advice?"

"Without hesitation." His smile remained in place. "Will you take a piece of advice from me?"

"And what would that be?"

"That we wash and put on clean clothes before we see her. Will you follow my advice?'

Wilford laughed. "Without hesitation, my friend. Without hesitation."

Still smiling, Lenard walked beside his friend, heading for the castle. He couldn't wait to see Della's expression when she learned her brother was still alive. His smile faltered slightly as he thought of his own brothers, imprisoned by the King. He pushed them from his thoughts, not about to let them ruin his day. He tilted his head back slightly, catching glimpses of the castle through the trees. Never could he have imagined his life would lead him there. He owed everything to Wilford.

He looked towards his friend. "I'll never be able to thank you enough for all you've done."

"I did very little. I only offered you some advice. The same advice I tried to offer your brothers. You were the one who decided to follow it." Wilford grinned, his teeth extremely white compared to the blood smeared across his face. "I am the one who can never thank you enough."

Lenard chuckled, coming to a stop so he could face his friend. "Obviously we're equally grateful."

Wilford nodded. "Now that, I can agree with."

"Let's get cleaned up so you can

see Della." At Wilford's nod, Lenard strode beside him towards the castle. He couldn't wait. Della was going to be extremely surprised.

Free Ebook

Subscribe to Avril's newsletter and receive a free ebook. This ebook is exclusive to those on her mailing list. To find out more about this offer visit:

www.avrilsabine.com/free-ebook

*

We value your privacy and will not sell, rent, exchange or loan your email address to third parties. Your information is confidential and you are under no obligation to remain on the mailing list and can unsubscribe at any time.

To The Reader

If you enjoyed this book, why not consider leaving a review to help other readers discover it too? Reader engagement is one of the few ways that lets an author know readers want more books in a particular series or genre. So leave a review and tell friends, not only about this book but also about other ones you've enjoyed, so you can continue to enjoy books by your favourite authors for years to come.

Dreams are meant to be lived,

Avril.

About The Author

Avril is an Australian author who lives with her family on acreage in South East Queensland. She writes mostly young adult and children's speculative fiction, but has been known to dabble in other genres. You can find more information about her at www.avrilsabine.com where you can also subscribe to her newsletter to be kept informed about new releases, current projects, blog posts and exclusive news.

Titles By Avril Sabine

Stories about strong characters and characters who discover their strengths.

Book 4: King's Request

Dragon Blood- Young Adult Urban Fantasy (with elements of romance)

(5 book series)

Book 1: Pliethin

Book 2: Wyvern

Book 3: Surety

Book 4: Knight

Book 5: Mage

Dragon Mage- Young Adult Urban Fantasy (with elements of romance)

(Series two of Dragon Blood series)

Book 1: Promise

Dragon Blood Chronicles- Young Adult Urban Fantasy (with elements of romance)

(Companion stand alone series to Dragon Blood)

Book 1: Oath

Book 2: Betrayed

Guardians Of The Round Table- Young Adult Fantasy LitRPG

(Co-written with Storm and Rhys Petersen)

Book 1: Dexterity Fail

Book 2: Goblin Boots

Book 3: Singed Feathers

Book 4: Frog Mage

Book 5: Crystal Mine

Book 6: Cursed Harp

Book 7: Treasure Seeker

Rosie's Rangers- Young Adult Western Steampunk

(6 book series)

Book 1: Justice

Book 2: Vengeance

Book 3: Treachery

Book 4: Accused

Book 5: Wanted

Book 6: Corruption

Mark Of Kings- Children's Fantasy

(Upper middle grade/preteen)

(4 book series)

Book 1: The Arena

Book 2: The Island

Book 3: The Assassin

Book 4: The King

STAND ALONE SERIES

Demon Hunters- Young Adult Urban Fantasy/Horror (with elements of romance)

Book 1: Blood Sacrifice

Book 2: Retribution

Book 3: Tainted

Book 4: Premonition

Book 5: Cursed

Book 6: Feud

Book 7: Extrication

Plea Of The Damned- Young Adult Urban Fantasy/Paranormal

(6 book series)

Book 1: Forgive Me Lucy

Book 2: Forgive Me Aiden

Book 3: Forgive Me Jena

Book 4: Forgive Me Kobe

Book 5: Forgive Me Marti

Book 6: Forgive Me Dawson

Realms Of The Fae- Young Adult Urban Fantasy (with elements of romance)

The Sword (short story in Like A Girl Anthology)

Heart Of Stone

Book 1: A Debt Owed

Book 2: Marked By The Hunt

Book 3: The Magic Collector

Book 4: An Unexpected Betrayal

Book 5: Imprisoned By Iron

Fairytales Retold (Short Stories)

Snow-White And Rose-Red

The Twelve Brothers

The Light Princess

Beauty And The Beast

Sleeping Beauty

Aschenputtel

The Golden Bird

The Frog Prince

The Death Of Koshchei The Deathless

Myths And Legends Retold (Short Stories)

Ion, Son Of Apollo

Sir Gawain And The Maid With The Narrow Sleeves

Princess Ilse, The Giant's Daughter

YOUNG ADULT NOVELS

Young Adult Fantasy (with elements of romance)

Elf Sight

Earth Bound

Young Adult Urban Fantasy

Stone Warrior (with elements of romance)

The Jungle Inside

Young Adult Contemporary (with elements of romance)

Through Your Eyes

The Ugly Stepsister

Perfect Little Princess

Young Adult Contemporary/ Paranormal

Whispers In The Dark (with elements of romance and same sex relationships)

Over Too Soon (with elements of romance)

Young Adult Sci-Fi

Experiment X-One-Six (Urban Sci-Fi/Superheroes)

An Endless Dawn (Post Apocalyptic Sci-Fi)

CHILDREN'S BOOKS

Dragon Lord (Preteen/early teens) (Fantasy)

The Irish Wizard (Upper middle grade) (Urban Fantasy)

SHORT STORIES

Urban Fantasy

Eternally Late

Dealings With Joe

Glimpses (short story in That Moment When Anthology)

Contemporary

The Brat Next Door

Fantasy LitRPG

(Set in the same world as Guardians Of The Round Table Series)

Tales Of Inadon 1: The Disc (Co-written with Storm and Rhys Petersen) (short story in Game On! Anthology)

Post Apocalyptic Sci-Fi

Compulsive Directive

NONFICTION

A Year Of Weekly Writing Exercises (Creative Writing)

Cooking For Families With Allergies (Cooking) (Co-written with Storm Petersen)

Tell Me A Story, Grandma (Memoir)

For the most up to date details on available titles visit:

www.avrilsabine.com/books/bibliography

Disclaimer

This is a work of fiction. Names, characters, businesses, places, events and incidents are either the products of the author's imagination or used in a fictitious manner. Any resemblance to actual persons, living or dead, or actual events is purely coincidental. The opinions expressed or beliefs held are those of the characters and should not be assumed to be the opinions or beliefs of the author.